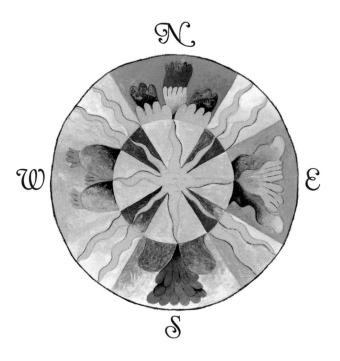

For DLB and
JMW and
all the small ones.

ABOUT THIS BOOK

The illustrations for this book were done in gouache and pencil on watercolor paper. This book was edited by Andrea Spooner, art directed by David Caplan, and designed by Prashansa Thapa. The production was supervised by Virginia Lawther, and the production editor was Jake Regier. The text was set in Bembo, and the display type is hand lettered.

The Wind & the Clover

AUDREY
HELEN
WEBER

LB
Little, Brown and Company
New York   Boston

More things than you can imagine
live in this field of clover,
but this is a story about the bees.

These bees.

These bees sleep in little holes.

They sleep all morning.
They dream until the sun comes...

...and then they play until it goes away.

The winds blow all night,

from near and far.

More days than you can imagine
 go by just like this,
  but this is a story about something different.

One morning,

one bee,

this bee,

dreamt of someplace different
and woke before the sun came.

Then the wind blew *north*, near and far.

So, she followed it.

The next morning,

one bee,

this bee,

dreamt a different dream
and woke before the sun came.

Then the wind blew *west*, near and far.

So, she followed it.

The next morning,

one bee,

this bee,

dreamt a different dream
and woke before the sun came.

Then the wind blew *south*, near and far.

So, she followed it.

The next morning,

one bee,

this bee,

dreamt a different dream
and woke before the sun came.

Then the wind blew *east*, near and far.

So, she followed it.

Just about as many mornings as you can imagine went by just like this.

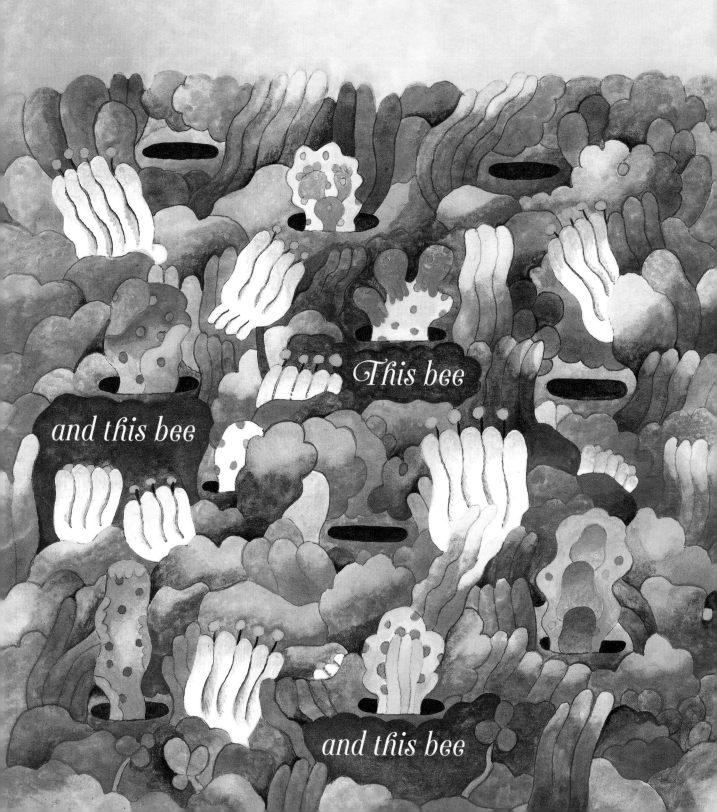

and all the rest

       dreamt of someplace different

           and followed the wind in directions

               we haven't even named yet...

...to places no one has ever seen.

Only one bee,

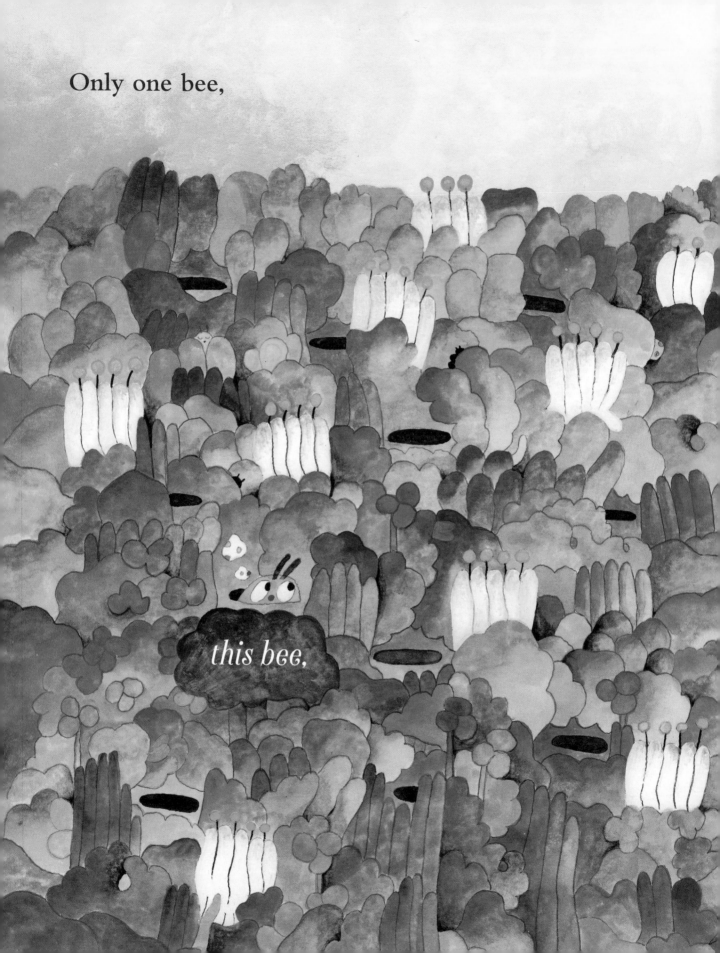

this bee,

dreamt the same dream
and slept in the same hole,
day after day.
But one calm morning,
she woke before the sun...

...and as the
light grew near,

she saw them.

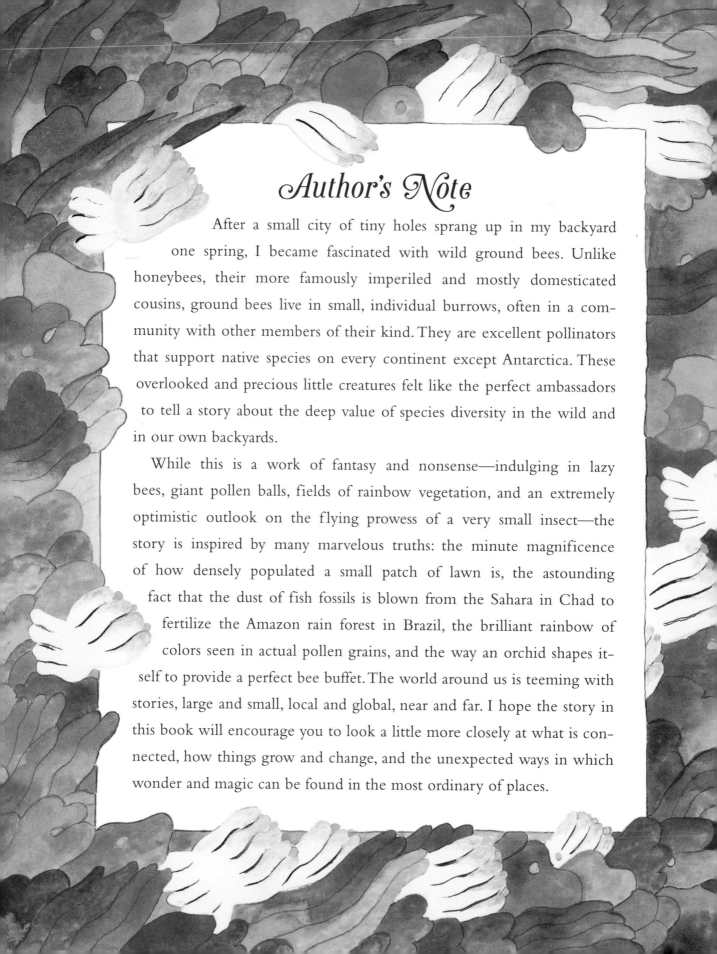

Author's Note

After a small city of tiny holes sprang up in my backyard one spring, I became fascinated with wild ground bees. Unlike honeybees, their more famously imperiled and mostly domesticated cousins, ground bees live in small, individual burrows, often in a community with other members of their kind. They are excellent pollinators that support native species on every continent except Antarctica. These overlooked and precious little creatures felt like the perfect ambassadors to tell a story about the deep value of species diversity in the wild and in our own backyards.

While this is a work of fantasy and nonsense—indulging in lazy bees, giant pollen balls, fields of rainbow vegetation, and an extremely optimistic outlook on the flying prowess of a very small insect—the story is inspired by many marvelous truths: the minute magnificence of how densely populated a small patch of lawn is, the astounding fact that the dust of fish fossils is blown from the Sahara in Chad to fertilize the Amazon rain forest in Brazil, the brilliant rainbow of colors seen in actual pollen grains, and the way an orchid shapes itself to provide a perfect bee buffet. The world around us is teeming with stories, large and small, local and global, near and far. I hope the story in this book will encourage you to look a little more closely at what is connected, how things grow and change, and the unexpected ways in which wonder and magic can be found in the most ordinary of places.